HIPPO POTTO & MOUSE

Roger Hargreaves

Publishers • GROSSET & DUNLAP • New York

Library of Congress Catalog Card Number: 81-84544
ISBN: 0-448-12315-0

First published in Great Britain by Hodder and Stoughton.
Published in the United States by Ottenheimer Publishers, Inc.
Published simultaneously in Canada.

HIPPO
POTTO
& MOUSE

If you come out of your house, turn left, and walk for nine hundred and ninety-nine miles, you will come to a house. Or rather a cottage. Christmas Cottage!

And in Christmas Cottage live those three very good friends—Hippo, Potto, and Mouse.

Hippo is a particularly earnest fellow. He goes to work every day in order to earn enough money so that he and Potto and Mouse can live very well.

Hippo worries a lot about money. In fact, he worries a lot about everything.

Probably Hippo wouldn't worry quite so much if it wasn't for Potto. Potto the playboy!
Potto is, and he wouldn't deny it, rather extravagant, to say the least. He likes to buy things.
If Potto had his way he'd buy everything there was in the world! The things
Potto buys.
No wonder
Hippo worries.

The third person who lives at Christmas Cottage is
Mouse. Mouse is a schoolboy. Or perhaps we should say
a schoolmouse. A mischievous schoolmouse. Or perhaps
we should say a naughty schoolmouse. The naughty
things Mouse does. No wonder Hippo worries.

One day while Hippo was at work,
and Mouse was at school,
Potto decided to go out for lunch.
So off into Town he went.
He selected the best table in the best
restaurant in the best hotel in Town
and had himself quite a lunch . . .
quite a lunch!

Potto ate a dozen jam tarts, and he drank four bottles of lemon.
Then Potto smiled a contented Potto smile.
"Waiter," he called. The waiter came up to the table.
"Would you like your bill, Sir?" he asked.
"No," replied Potto, "I would like second helpings."
And he had the same again!
"Waiter," he wheezed, feeling a little, if not a lot, full.
"Would you like your bill now, Sir?" asked the waiter.
"No," wheezed Potto, "I would like some ice cream!"

After lunch Potto walked down High Street. Well, we
say walked, but actually it was much more of a waddle.
He waddled down High Street, and over the bridge,
and along the road, and eventually he came to an airfield.
And there, in the middle of the airfield, stood something
that caught Potto's eye.
A beautiful shiny bright red airplane.
"Ooo," said Potto. "Ooo yes!"

man came up.

"Are you interested in airplanes?" he asked Potto.

"Do I look like the sort of a person who would NOT be interested in airplanes?" said Potto.

"Well, no," replied the man. "But would you be interested in buying this one by any chance? It is for sale!"

"Ooo," said Potto. "Ooo yes!"

Potto climbed up into the cockpit of the airplane and started the engine.
"Do you know how to fly an airplane?" asked the man.
"Do I look like the sort of person who does NOT know how to fly an airplane?" said Potto.

looked down at the man.
end the bill to Mr. Hippo at Christmas
ttage," he said and took off.

"Whee," shouted Potto as he flew through the air.
"Wheeeee," shouted Potto as he flew through a cloud.
Far below him he spied the schoolhouse.
"I know," he chortled, "I'll pick Mouse up from school."

Potto landed in the playground just as Mouse came out of school.
"Wow," remarked Mouse.
"Hop in," said Potto.

"Well, Mouse. What do you think?" called Potto over his shoulder. "Great," shouted Mouse at the top of his squeak as the wind whistled between his ears.

And on they flew. Potto and Mouse in their beautiful shiny bright red airplane.

Hippo was hard at work in his office.

"Time to go home soon," he thought, "and cook supper for Potto and Mouse."

He glanced out of his office window.

"Good Heavens," he gasped.

"Hello, Hippo," boomed Potto as he flew past the office window.

Hippo went white.

Poor Hippo grabbed his hat and ran out of his office and
all the way back to Christmas Cottage.
Potto had landed the airplane in the garden.
"Quite a surprise, don't you agree?"
he said, as Hippo came puffing up the garden path.

"But where did you get it?" sputtered Hippo.
"Bought it," replied Potto.
"But we can't possibly afford an airplane," said Hippo.
"Nonsense," said Potto.
"But how much did it cost?" asked Hippo.
"Oh, not very much," replied Potto, "not very much at all. In fact, I didn't even bother to ask!"
Hippo was speechless.

Later that evening a discussion took place.
"Why can't I keep it?" cried Potto for the hundredth time. "Oh, please let me keep it. Please please please please please please."
"No!" said Hippo.
"But," said Potto.
"No!" said Hippo.
"Please?" said Mouse.
"No!" said Hippo.
"Tomorrow you will take it back!"
"But," said Potto.
"No!" said Hippo.
"And that's final!"

The following day Hippo telephoned from his office. "Well, Potto," he said, "did you do it? Have you taken it back?"

"Yes," replied Potto grumpil[...] "Thank goodness," Hippo sai[...] and put down the telephone. He heaved a sigh of relief an[...] got on with his work.

That evening Hippo walked slowly home from work.
"Perhaps I have been a little hard on Potto," he thought
himself. "But it really is for his own good!"
e walked wearily through the garden gate.
Oh, no!" he gasped.
nd what do you think he saw standing outside
hristmas Cottage?

The longest, most powerful, gleaming, shining automobile. "Hello, Hippo," shouted Potto, sitting behind the wheel of the car and laughing. "Surprise. Surprise!"
Oh, Potto!